TECH GIRLS™

Careers for TECH GIRLS IN AUDIO ENGINEERING

JACKSON NIEUWLAND

Rosen YA™
New York

Published in 2019 by The Rosen Publishing Group, Inc.
29 East 21st Street, New York, NY 10010

First Edition

Library of Congress Cataloging-in-Publication Data

Names: Nieuwland, Jackson, author.
Title: Careers for Tech Girls in Audio Engineering / Jackson Nieuwland.
Description: New York: Rosen Publishing, 2019 | Series: Tech Girls | Includes bibliographical references and index. | Audience: Grades 7–12.
Identifiers: LCCN 2017059606| ISBN 9781508180081 (library bound) | ISBN 9781508180098 (pbk.)
Subjects: LCSH: Sound—Recording and reproducing—Vocational guidance—Juvenile literature. | Women in engineering—Juvenile literature. | Sound engineers—Juvenile literature.
Classification: LCC TK7881.4 .N495 2019 | DDC 621.389/3023—dc23
LC record available at https://lccn.loc.gov/2017059606

Manufactured in the United States of America

CONTENTS

Introduction

When you go to a concert, the music doesn't travel directly from the band's instruments to your ears. It comes from the instruments and is picked up by microphones and converted into an electric signal. This signal is run through a mixing desk to balance the levels, then through an amplifier to strengthen the signal, and finally it comes through the loudspeakers, which convert the signal back into sound energy for the audience. When you watch a movie, the soundtrack isn't just whatever music they had playing in the background while they were filming. It is recorded separately. Then during postproduction, different audio layers are added for dialogue, music, and sound effects. These processes are the responsibility of audio engineers. Now you might be asking, what exactly is an audio engineer?

Well, you know how in music videos, when they show a shot of the recording studio and there are those desks with hundreds

The image of an audio engineer sitting behind a mixing desk has been popularized by music videos and movies, but not many people actually understand what the job entails.

of knobs and sliders on them? The people sitting at those desks are audio engineers. Or how about at the beginning of a song, when the singer asks someone to turn their vocals up? The singer is talking to the audio engineer. To put it simply, an audio engineer's job is to set up, manage, and operate the technology necessary to record, mix, and reproduce sound. This can be as easy as putting a microphone in front of someone and hitting the big red button or as complicated as installing a public announcement system throughout an entire university or government building.

Most people think of audio engineering in relation to music, but the truth is that fields as diverse as television, video games, professional sports, and podcasting all require audio engineers, so there are a wide range of job opportunities in the field. If you decide to pursue a career in audio engineering, the specific elements of the profession you decide to specialize in will determine what sort of environment you will be working in. You could be touring with a theater production or recording conference calls in an office. You could be operating the sound system at an auction house or working at a radio station, making sure the presenters can hear what they sound like.

Unfortunately, as in so many tech industries, women are underrepresented in audio engineering. Based on estimates by the Audio Engineering Society (AES) Women in Audio Committee, less than 5 percent of people working in the audio engineering industry were female in 2000. Regrettably, that committee no longer exists. According to a 2016 survey by the AES, only 7 percent of its members were women.

However, times are changing, and a number of trailblazing women are paving the way for more women in the audio engineering field. Women like Shani Gandhi, Karrie Keyes, Ai-Ling Lee, and Karen Kane have made their mark in audio engineering history, and that list is only going to grow with time. Perhaps you could be part of it one day.

Chapter one

WHAT IS AUDIO ENGINEERING?

Audio engineers aren't the only people who work with sound for a living. There are musicians, producers, developers, composers, sound designers, and more. Sometimes these roles overlap, and some people move between these roles throughout their careers, but they all have different focuses and requirements. Let's take a look at the specific things audio engineers do that separate them from all those other jobs.

ARE YOU A FUTURE AUDIO ENGINEER?

Do you enjoy setting up the sound systems for your friends' parties? Do you notice when a venue has poor acoustics? Is the audio quality of music important to you? Do you hear details in recordings that other people don't seem to notice? Then you've probably got what it takes to become an audio engineer. But having the right interests and

If you enjoy setting up the sound systems for parties, you may be considering a career in audio engineering. While DJing is not the same as engineering, both involve mixing.

a bit of natural talent doesn't necessarily equal a successful career.

If you really want to become an audio engineer, you'll need to be willing to commit years of your life to learning and improving your craft and establishing yourself in the industry. You can start working on this today by joining your school's radio station or audiovisual club. After high school, you will need to obtain a degree or certificate in audio engineering, recording arts, broadcasting technology, or a similar discipline, as well as learning on your own time by researching new technology and techniques and practicing on your personal equipment. Once you're qualified and ready to work, you will probably have to start off by taking unpaid gigs and internships before becoming an assistant engineer and eventually specializing in a certain aspect of audio engineering.

THE LIFE OF AN AUDIO ENGINEER

Being an audio engineer means living a different lifestyle from an office worker, a schoolteacher, or most other occupations. The biggest difference is the hours you work. Whether you're employed at a recording studio, on a film set, or doing sound for a touring band, you're unlikely to be working nine to five. When they're in the creative zone, musicians like to record all through the night, the workday on a film set doesn't end until all of that day's scenes have been completed, and concerts don't typically take place while the sun is still up. So you need to be flexible with your availability and willing to work long hours, which can impact the rest of your life. For instance, it can be hard to have a social life when you're not available to hang out at the same time as anyone else. But that doesn't mean you won't have human interaction. You may find you spend a lot of time with big personalities—musicians and directors who have very specific visions of how they want their projects to sound. As an audio engineer, your job isn't just to manage the audio—you also need to manage the people behind the sound, using your technical expertise to translate their visions into a finished product.

THE SKILLS OF AN AUDIO ENGINEER

To be a competent audio engineer, there are a variety of different skills you need to develop. As you continue in your career, you might pick one as a special area of focus, but it's always useful to at least have a foundation of knowledge in every aspect of the profession. If you want to have your own studio one day, you'll need to be able to oversee the entire process.

We all know what recording is: you put a microphone up to a sound and capture it, allowing you to play it back. But being a professional recording engineer means knowing the differences between digital and analogue recording, setting up and properly placing microphones, operating computer programs like Pro Tools and Ableton, and much more.

Mixing is the art of combining multiple sound files into a single track. For example, mixing a song involves taking the recordings of each individual instrument and vocalist and layering them together so that no one part overwhelms or drowns out the others and then adding any additional effects.

Mastering is the final step of preparing a collection of audio for reproduction, be it an album, an audiobook, or a television soundtrack. The mastering engineer works with the mixed material, equalizing the audio between tracks, setting peak limits, creating fades-in and -out, editing minor flaws, compressing the files, and handling countless other small details.

The number of knobs and sliders on a mixing desk can be intimidating, but a good audio engineer knows exactly what each one does and when to use it.

Working with live sound requires elements of all of these skills as well as knowledge of acoustics, operation of monitors, power handling of speakers, and the ability to fix problems and adjust at a moment's notice.

WHERE DO AUDIO ENGINEERS WORK?

While audio engineers are required in almost every industry, there are a few fields that employ the vast majority of audio engineers. According to a 2016 report by the Bureau of Labor Statistics (BLS), almost 60 percent of sound engineering technicians were employed in either music, film, or television and radio. Due to changes in the way we consume our media, more and more audio engineers are likely to be working in newer media platforms such as podcasts, audiobooks, and video games.

MUSIC

Music is the first industry that comes to mind when most people think about audio engineering, and with good reason: according to the BLS's 2016 figures, audio engineers make up over 18 percent of the industry's employment, which is far more than in any other industry. This makes sense, seeing as music is an auditory medium. Audio engineers working in the music industry are involved in various stages of the creative process, including recording, mixing, mastering, and live performances.

FILM

While the music industry may be made up of a higher percentage of audio engineers, the film industry employs more audio engineers overall, with 4,490 workers, compared to the music industry's 3,150, in 2016. In addition to working on feature films, these engineers also work on trailers, short films, and straight-to-DVD or streaming releases. Working in film as an audio engineer can include a wide variety of jobs, including recording dialogue, scores, and sound

People usually think of film as a visual art form, but recording the audio can sometimes be more challenging than capturing the images.

effects, dubbing, mixing, mastering, and sound design and editing.

BROADCAST: TV AND RADIO

Although the broadcast industry doesn't employ as many audio engineers as the music and film industries do, television and radio broadcasting is still a viable career path for audio engineers. For instance, if you want to use your audio skills in news media, then broadcasting is definitely the way to go. Working in broadcasting is different from film and music recording because it's a live medium. This means there is less room for error as you can't go back and fix your mistakes later. To work in this industry, you need to be able to solve problems and perform under pressure.

NEW MEDIA

As technology continues to develop, more opportunities for audio engineers are created. Twenty years ago, podcasts didn't exist; now, 24 percent of Americans listen to podcasts on a monthly basis, according to a 2017 study by Edison Research and Triton Digital. While sales of physical books continue to decrease, audiobooks are thriving thanks to the success of services like Audible. A 2016 survey by the Audio Publishers Association found that audiobook sales increased by 18.2 percent over 2015 for an estimated total of $2.1 billion. Meanwhile, video games become more and more advanced every year, requiring more sound effects and voice actors, which of course means more work for audio engineers. With all these changes, we can't predict what new mediums we'll be using in the future, but audio engineers will always be needed to facilitate them.

Chapter two

GETTING THE BAND HEARD

If you're interested in becoming an audio engineer, chances are that you like music, so where better to work than in the music industry? It's a place where you can turn your passion into a living wage. But just deciding you want to work in music isn't specific enough. There are many parts to the creative process of engineering sound, and most engineers specialize in just one of them.

RECORDING

When it comes to audio, nothing is ever as simple as it seems. You would think that recording an album would just be a case of playing the music into a microphone, but that's just the first step, and even that step is more complicated than you'd expect.

TRACKING

Tracking—the step of actually recording the audio—is almost always the most time-consuming part of the production process. This is because, unlike at a live

This might be what you imagine when you think of a band recording a song, but in reality each instrument is usually recorded individually.

performance, in a studio recording the aim is to make every element of a song perfect. In order to achieve this, each instrument is recorded separately over the course of multiple takes. The tracking engineer's role is to select and set up microphones for each instrument, taking into account the acoustics of the room, the sound frequency of the instrument, and the effect the musician and producer are aiming for; monitor the recording, giving feedback on takes and weighing in on whether more are required; and splicing together the best parts of several takes to create the perfect track. Because this process is so time consuming, it can take hours or even days to record a three- or four-minute song.

MIXING

Once all the separate instruments of a song have been recorded, the mixing engineer steps in to layer them together into a complete song. The volume of each track needs to be regulated so that they all blend together smoothly, and no one instrument drowns out any of the others. Audio can be mixed in either mono (where the same audio comes from all speakers), stereo (where the audio is split between left and right), or surround sound (where there are four or more audio channels). Mixing is also the step during which effects like Auto-Tune, reverb, compression, and panning (specifying which speaker or headphone specific parts of a song are played from) are added to the audio. Mixing is often underappreciated because when it's done well, nobody should notice it.

MASTERING

Mastering engineers put the finishing touches on the album. Their job is to make sure all the songs are in the same volume range and that they flow together seamlessly. They remove any clicks, pops, or other imperfections in the audio that were missed in the earlier steps, set volume limits to prevent distortion, create the fade-ins and fade-outs between songs, and test the sound on multiple types of speakers and headphones to make sure it sounds just as good on all platforms. Once they're done, the album is ready for reproduction on compact disc, vinyl, or—most often these days—digital format.

SHANI GANDHI: A TRAILBLAZER IN MUSIC ENGINEERING

At just twenty-nine years old, Shani Gandhi is already a star of the music-engineering field. She has already won a Best Folk Album Grammy for her work on Sarah Jarosz's *Undercurrent*, and she was nominated for the Best Engineered Album, Non-Classical award for her work on the same album. She was also the first female engineer to mix a *Billboard* chart-topping country single, with "Peter Pan" by Kelsea Ballerini. She studied at Ithaca College in Ithaca, New York, where she earned a bachelor of music degree in performance and sound recording technology. She was the first woman to graduate from the program. She now lives in Nashville, Tennessee, where she has worked with acclaimed metal and country music producers Gary Paczosa and Michael Wagener.

Gandhi has faced discrimination in the male-dominated engineering industry, often being mistaken for a personal assistant or losing out on jobs to her male peers. She puts a positive spin on this situation, saying, "If they're going to hold me to a higher standard because I'm young and a female, that's

(continued on the next page)

(continued from the previous page)

Grammy Award–winning audio engineer Shani Gandhi appears here with her mentor and collaborator Gary Paczosa at an event honoring Jack White.

fine with me. Hold me to a higher standard. I'll meet you there." In fact, she credits a lot of her success to the challenges she's faced. When someone else gets an engineering job she wanted and she thinks that person has done well with it, she says that she'll "go to them and ask, 'How did you do that?'" Now a lot of people are starting to ask her the same question.

LIVE MUSIC

Like recording an album, you wouldn't expect the preparations for a concert to be all that involved. You'd think it would just mean plugging in the instruments and playing, but, of course, there's a lot more to it than that. There are three main aspects of live music engineering: setup and sound check, mixing, and monitors.

Long before the doors open and the audience starts arriving, there is work to be done. Microphones need to be placed, wired, assigned to channels, and tested, as do electric instruments like guitars or keyboards. Then it's time for the sound check itself. Each instrument and vocalist plays into his or her microphone individually, so that the engineer can set the levels for both the house speakers and the monitors. Then they all play together so the engineer can do a preliminary mix.

Mixing live music involves constraints that you don't have to deal with when working on studio recordings. The most obvious of these is time. When you're mixing a recorded song, you can play each track back as many times as you need to get the balance right. At a live gig, you have to figure it out on the fly, fixing problems and correcting mistakes as they come up. No matter how well you prepared prior to the show, there will always be things that you need to deal with. You're also limited by the venue's setup. If the room has poor acoustics, you can't make structural changes or move to a different location. You just have to work with what you're given. This also applies to the equipment you have to work with. If the venue's mixing desk only has eight channels, you won't be able to mix as precisely.

The audience members aren't the only ones who need to hear the music at a concert. The band needs to be able to hear what they're doing as well. The speakers that play the sound back to the performers are called monitors. Monitor engineers do essentially the same thing as live mixing engineers, except they're preparing the sound for the musicians, rather than the audience.

PREPARATION

Music engineers aren't (necessarily) musicians or producers, but because they work with them closely, they need to understand the terms and language they use. This means that even if you don't have aspirations to be a rock star, you may want to take guitar, piano, or drumming lessons so you can learn more about music itself.

As well as learning to play instruments, you should be taking every possible opportunity to get involved with other aspects of music. Join your school's audiovisual (AV) club, see if you can do sound for the school play or your friends' bands, or volunteer at tech expos. "You're not getting paid, but you're demonstrating your work ethic and they'll remember that. Create those relationships," says recording engineer Lenise Bent. "People will remember you. … I'll have some people in my head when someone calls me for a recommendation for an entry-level position."

Once you've finished high school, further study can set you up for a career in music engineering. Many universities with music degrees offer programs in engineering or recording technology, and community and technical colleges often provide certificates in audio production and engineering. These sorts of qualifications show potential employers that you are committed to working in this field and that you have a strong base of knowledge to build on.

JOB OUTLOOK

There is a well-established pathway to becoming a fully fledged studio engineer. Most people start out as either an intern or apprentice for an established engineer, eventually working their way up to becoming an assistant engineer, and then finally becoming an engineer in their own right. While

Karrie Keyes gives a speech at the 2017 She Rocks Awards in Anaheim, California. Keyes has been the sound engineer for the band Pearl Jam since 1992.

you don't need a degree or certificate to begin this process, many employers look for candidates with postsecondary school education. Some courses even offer an internship as part of the program.

Finding employment in live music engineering can be more difficult as people often hire engineers based on whom they know, without a formal application process. That's why networking is so important in this industry. On the plus side, because of the strong relationships artists often form with their live engineers, once you do find a job and gain your employer's trust, you tend have great job security. One great example of this is Karrie Keyes, who has been Pearl Jam's monitor engineer for twenty-five years. If you can get a gig that lasts that long, you'll be doing pretty well for yourself.

According to a Bureau of Labor Statistics report, there were 3,150 sound engineers employed in the music industry in 2016, making up 18.49 percent of the industry as a whole. The number of jobs in the field was expected to rise by 13 percent by 2026, which is a higher-than-average increase. So if working in the music industry is your dream, now is the time to start working on making it a reality!

Chapter three

MOVIES AREN'T SILENT ANYMORE

Although the music industry is the first thing most people think of when they hear the term audio engineer, the film industry actually employs more audio engineers overall. Making a film can be a huge production, Hollywood films create thousands of jobs each year, and according to the Bureau of Labor Statistics, just over 1 percent of people working in the film industry were audio engineers in 2016, amounting to a total of 4,490 audio engineers.

PRODUCTION

Very little of the sound you hear when you watch a movie is recorded at the same time as the visuals. Dialogue is the main form of audio that gets recorded on set for use in the final film, and even that is sometimes rerecorded in postproduction. But that doesn't mean audio engineers aren't necessary during the filming of a movie.

Boom microphone operators don't get a lot of attention, even though their job is difficult, because if they're doing it well, no one notices they're there.

In order to record the dialogue and other necessary audio during filming, sound technicians use a variety of specialty microphones. These include lavalier microphones, which are small and clip, unseen, onto an actor's clothing to capture a specific character's dialogue, and directional, or "shotgun," microphones, which only pick up sound from the front, allowing filmmakers to cut out the majority of background noise during recording.

AI-LING LEE: THERE'S A FIRST TIME FOR EVERYTHING

Ai-Ling Lee has come a long way since beginning her career working on commercials for a small TV studio in Singapore. She moved to Los Angeles in 1998, at the age of nineteen, without a job offer. Since then, she has worked on many successful movies, including *The Twilight Saga: New Moon*, *Tangled*, and *Deadpool*.

Lee received the most recognition for her work on the 2016 film *La La Land*, for which she did sound mixing and sound editing. She received Oscar nominations for both categories, making her the first Asian woman to be recognized for sound editing. She and her collaborator Mildred Iatrou Morgan were also the first all-female team to be nominated for sound mixing.

Lee is happy to see more women beginning to work in audio. "Over the years, I'm seeing more and more young women coming out from film school who are actually interested in sound design or sound mixing, and that's a really, really good thing." Her advice for those women is, "Keep trying. Keep working hard to prove yourself. In this field, it's all about word of mouth and recommendations. Keep working hard and soon someone will notice."

Directional and more standard microphones are often mounted on a boom for filming. A boom is a pole used to hold a microphone as close to the actors as possible without it getting in the shot. Boom operators have a physically demanding job, having to hold microphones in position through long takes and sometimes having to move them to follow the actors.

Another important part of creating audio for a scene is recording the room tone. This simply means recording the sound in the room when no one is speaking or doing anything else noisy. This audio can then be layered in the background of any dialogue or other sound that needs to be added in postproduction so that it flows seamlessly with the audio that was recorded on site.

The mixing desks used for engineering film audio can be even larger than those used for recording music because of the huge scale of movie productions.

POSTPRODUCTION

Postproduction is when the audio side of movies gets interesting. Postproduction includes everything that happens once the filming is completed, and it usually takes much longer than the filming itself. Postproduction work can involve a large team of sound people and the tasks include everything from creating sound effects, to mixing the audio for the entire film, and a lot more in between.

DESIGN

Dialogue isn't the only thing you hear when you're watching a movie. Sound design is the process of sourcing and creating the sound effects that you hear in films. This includes sounds like explosions, thunder, and breaking glass, as well as any music that appears in the film, and Foley. Named after the sound effects artist Jack Foley, Foley refers to human-based sound effects, like footsteps or a punch in the face. Foley artists often reenact entire scenes with microphones set up to record their bodily movements rather than their speech.

The design phase is also when additional dialogue is recorded. This process is called automatic dialogue replacement (ADR) and is used to replace low-quality audio or to add new dialogue to scenes. Often, when recording ADR, actors will watch the footage of the scene in order to lip-synch with their performance as closely as possible.

EDITING

Once all the audio for a film has been gathered, a sound editor pieces it all together into a cohesive soundtrack that makes sense alongside the visuals. This means matching the dialogue tracks to the takes the director has selected, syncing them with the visuals, cutting any unwanted audio, trimming the recordings to the required length, and placing the score and sound effects created in sound design into the soundtrack.

MIXING

Just like the songs on an album, the soundtrack of a movie needs to be mixed. Instead of instruments, the mixing engineer balances each actor's dialogue, the background music, the various room tones, and any sound effects. This stage also involves the equivalent of mastering for an album because although a movie isn't split into separate songs, the different scenes all need to be within the same volume range.

PREPARATION

Most people who work with sound in the film industry are film school graduates. Many programs offer degrees focusing on sound design, sound editing, and audio production. This is a good way to learn the skills required to get a job in the industry and acts as proof to employers that you know what you're doing and are committed to this career path.

Audio engineering isn't something you can learn to do just by reading about it. Hands-on experience is the most important part of learning the job.

But film school isn't the only place you can hone your skills. More general audio-engineering courses can also prepare you for a career in film audio. And with today's technology, it's never been easier to make your own movies. Working on every aspect of production will not only help you develop your talents for working with sound but also give you a better understanding of how audio fits in with the bigger picture of filmmaking. If you have friends who are also interested in film, offer to help with their projects, and offer your services as a volunteer for any local productions. Many successful audio engineers began at the bottom like this and worked their way up to high-level positions in the industry.

JOB OUTLOOK

According to the Bureau of Labor Statistics, the demand for sound-engineering technicians was expected to increase by 8 percent between 2016 and 2026, which is faster than the average rate for all jobs. Successful women in audio engineering, including Ai-Ling Lee, Mildred Iatrou Morgan, Becky Sullivan, and Karen Baker Landers, have all noted that more and more young women are entering the field. This is great news for girls who are considering a career in audio engineering. The more women there are in this traditionally male-dominated industry, the more welcoming it will be for the women who follow after them.

Chapter four

PUTTING SOUND ON THE AIRWAVES

Music and film aren't the only industries that hire audio engineers. Broadcasting has just as much, if not more, of a need for skilled audio professionals. While TV and radio have a lot in common with film and music, they also have their own unique collection of requirements and challenges.

RADIO

It makes sense that radio stations require audio engineers since, like music, radio is an entirely sound-based medium. Working in radio is similar in a lot of ways to working at a music venue, mixing live concerts. You set up and test microphones in the studio or on location; mix the audio on the fly, solving problems as they arise; and adjust the volume in the presenters' and guests' headphones, just as you would the monitors for a band.

The difference is in how the sound you're working with is transmitted. Instead of playing from speakers

Preparing a set for recording is a time-consuming process. Sometimes it takes even longer to set up than to do the recording itself.

on site, the audio is broadcast over radio waves to a much wider audience. This means you need to be familiar with broadcast technology, such as transmitters, and perform tasks, such as climbing antenna towers, that other audio engineers never have to think about.

Specializing in this type of engineering can help you reach heights that you never would have imagined. Marianna Woodson Cobb is a great example of this. She was one of only two female broadcasting engineers in the Washington, DC, area in the 1950s, and her work took her all the way to the top of the Empire State Building, where she was hired to install an antenna that would allow three radio stations to broadcast to the region. There aren't many jobs that provide you with experiences like that.

Installing microphones and speakers into football players' helmets in a way that they won't be damaged during the game is a challenging task for an audio engineer.

TV

Television broadcast engineering takes all the challenges of radio and adds to them. It turns out that synchronizing sound and visuals is more difficult than broadcasting audio on its own. Not only do television broadcast engineers have to mix audio live and work with transmitters and antennae, they are also responsible for more complicated editing, including dubbing, voiceovers, and adding sound effects such as laugh tracks.

Some television programs, like news and sporting event broadcasts, require large amounts of audio recording in the field, often in poor weather conditions or at venues with poor acoustics, which can make it challenging to capture high-quality audio. In these situations, audio engineers need to carefully select the right types of microphones and set them up in a way that minimizes background noise. On these types of jobs, the audio and visuals are transmitted live to the studio and then broadcast to the audience from there.

SHERRY KLEIN: FROM MUSIC TO TELEVISION

Sherry Klein grew up wanting to be a musician and studied music and composition in high school and at university. As she grew up, her interests shifted from playing music herself to the

(continued on the next page)

(continued from the previous page)

more technical side of audio. After she finished college, she began her career in audio as a recording engineer in Boston, beginning on the desk, handling phone calls, and working her way up the ladder, eventually moving to Los Angeles in the late 1970s, where she was one of only four female audio engineers working at the time.

In the mid-1980s, several record companies went bankrupt and Klein found she wasn't getting as much work, so when she was offered an opportunity to shift her focus to the television industry, she jumped at the chance and began working mixing TV shows immediately. As she continued working in the television industry, Klein began to specialize in mixing dialogue and was an early adopter of Pro Tools for mixing. She even left her position at Sony because they weren't ready to transition to the new technology.

Klein has since found success and recognition working in television. She has been nominated for two Primetime Emmy awards in Sound Mixing for her work on *Burn Notice*, as well as two Cinema Audio Society awards for *Nash Bridges* and *Jericho*. Other noteworthy shows she has worked on include *Dawson's Creek*, *Arrested Development*, *Sons of Anarchy*, *The Shield*, *Baywatch*, *The Killing*, and *This Is Us*. To other women aiming to become mixers, she says, "I think there are a lot more opportunities than ever before for women moving into mixing positions. … As far as getting into it and coming up through the channels, it's a long road. It's a very satisfying road. Ultimately, you do have to learn how to have your life, while still devoting the time needed to have the gig."

PREPARATION

If your school has its own radio station or if there's a local station you can volunteer for, that is the perfect place to start. There's no better way to learn a job than by doing it. High school classes in electronics, mathematics, film studies, and physics will also help you build up the knowledge base you'll need to learn the more advanced aspects of audio engineering.

Collaboration is a huge part of the job of an audio engineer. Learning as part of a group will help aspiring audio engineers to work well with other people.

Once you've finished high school, there are various paths you could take to become a broadcast engineer. You could begin working in a studio right away as a runner or in another entry-level position and learn from being in the environment, gradually working your way up. Or you could continue your education by pursuing an associate's degree in broadcasting or a bachelor's degree in engineering.

The Society of Broadcast Engineers also offers several noncompulsory certifications. These include certified audio engineer, certified professional broadcast engineer, and certified broadcast television engineer, among others. These certificates are available to nonmembers for a slightly higher fee and all require passing an exam. They prove to employers that you are a competent broadcasting professional who knows the industry standards and is committed to working in the field.

JOB OUTLOOK

The Bureau of Labor Statistics predicted that the number of jobs in the broadcast engineering field would decrease by 3 percent between 2016 and 2026. This is at least in part due to the increasing popularity of cable, satellite, and online streaming services, which require different skills and fewer people than traditional broadcasts. The BLS also reports that it is becoming more and more common for networks to broadcast multiple stations out of the same studio, allowing one engineer to do the work that was once split between a number of different people.

None of this means that the broadcast industry is disappearing. There are still expected to be 32,900 broadcast engineers working in the United States in 2026. But if it's your dream to work in broadcast television or radio, you might want to get in before the jobs start drying up any further. Otherwise, there are new mediums popping up with growing demand for audio engineers.

Chapter five

THE NEWEST SOUNDS

It seems safe to say that the demand for audio engineers will never dry up because whenever one industry that deals with sound goes into decline, a new one pops up. Three of the fresher markets for audio engineers are gaming, podcasts, and audiobooks.

GAMING

Audio has been a part of video games ever since the early games, like *Pong*, *Space Invaders*, and *Asteroids*, were released in the 1970s. As technology has advanced and games have become more complex and immersive (especially with the advent of virtual-reality gaming), audio has played a bigger and bigger role. Modern games often feature scores, sound effects, and an array of voice actors, reminiscent of movies.

The interactive nature of games calls for even more advanced audio cues and transitions than films use. Certain songs or sound effects will be triggered by the player performing a specific action in the game, and some dialogue will occur only if the player makes a certain set of decisions. Narrative games also often have a longer run time than movies,

Audio is an important tool for helping to make video games immersive. As video games become more complex, there will be an increased need for audio engineers.

meaning that more audio needs to be recorded, mixed, and synchronized to appear in the games. Not only do game soundtracks have a long run time, they can also have incredible detail, with sound designers often creating different background sounds for each setting in the game as well as for all the different objects in those settings.

EMILY RIDGWAY: PLAYING THE MUSIC SO YOU CAN PLAY THE GAMES

After growing up playing video games with her father, who was a programmer himself, Emily Ridgway began working in the video-game industry in 2003. During her final year of college, where she earned a bachelor's degree in music, specializing in music and sound for film, TV, and multimedia, she visited several video-game companies in her home country of Australia to see how they did things and express her interest in working in the industry. Nothing came of those visits right away, but six months later, Pandemic Studios offered her a job as a junior sound designer.

Since then, Ridgway has had a successful career, moving to the United States and working as an audio director for Irrational Games and a music director and lead sound designer for Double Fine Productions, among other positions. She has also set up her own game audio consultancy company, Emily Industries. Over the course of her career, Ridgway has worked on a number of high-profile games, including *Destroy All Humans*, *Costume Quest*, *Brutal Legend*, *and Bioshock.*

Ridgway has won many awards for her work, including the Australian Game Developer Conference Award for Best Game Audio for *Destroy All Humans*; the Academy of Interactive Arts and Sciences Award for Outstanding Achievement in Soundtrack for *Brutal Legend*; and more than ten separate awards for *Bioshock*. She has also had the chance to work closely with her childhood hero, Tim Schafer, whose games she grew up playing.

Video games are only becoming more advanced, as virtual-reality and augmented-reality technology push the boundaries of what was previously considered possible. As a result, there are a lot of exciting new opportunities in gaming for audio engineers to work on the cutting edge of sound and technology.

PODCASTS

Podcasts are audio series that automatically download new episodes to listeners' devices when they subscribe. They were invented in 2003 by Adam Curry but didn't gain wide popularity until iTunes

Emily Ridgway was the audio director for *Bioshock*, which won awards for Best Sound, Best Use of Licensed Music, Best Original Instrumental, Best Interactive Score, and more.

added podcast features in 2005. The word "podcast" is a combination of the words iPod and broadcast.

One of the great things about podcasts is their low barrier to entry. All you need to make a podcast is a computer and an internet connection. Of course, more serious podcasters often use more specialized microphones and some even record in professional

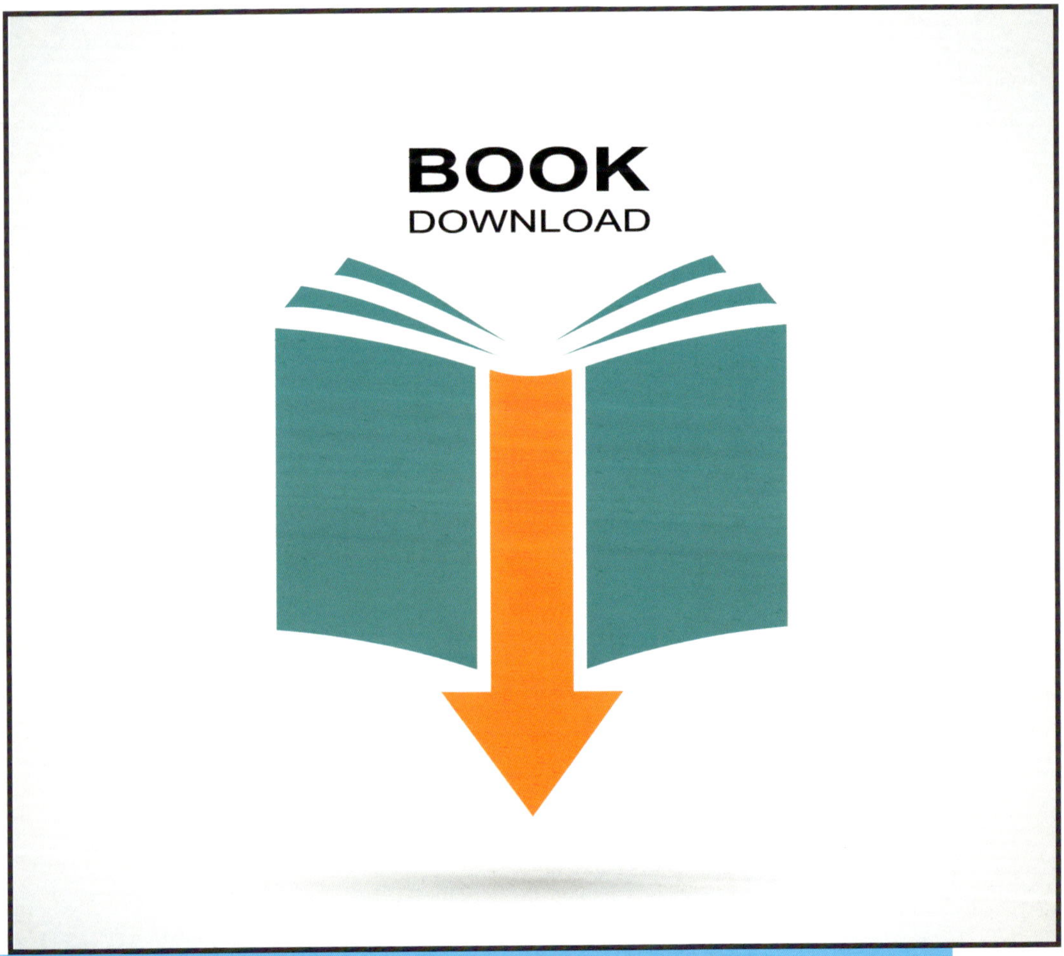

The popularity of audiobooks continues to grow and is driven in part by their accessibility online and on people's phones and tablets.

studios, but this isn't necessary to produce a podcast and build an audience. This means that podcasts aren't the biggest job market for audio engineers, even though they have become wildly popular, with almost a quarter of Americans listening to them on a monthly basis, according to a 2017 study by Edison Research.

The podcasts that create the most new audio-engineering jobs are those produced by already existing businesses or organizations that move into podcasting, like How Stuff Works and TED, as they need to employ engineers to produce their podcasts. On the other hand, with many radio and television stations beginning to release podcasts, some audio engineers who previously worked in broadcasting are now beginning to move into podcasting as part of their existing jobs.

AUDIOBOOKS

Audiobooks have been around for longer than video games and podcasts, but they have seen an increase in popularity since the success of Audible, Audiobooks.com, and other digital audiobook retailers. The Audio Publishers Association reported that audiobook sales increased by 18.2 percent in 2015, for a total of around $2.1 billion, 82.4 percent of which came from digital downloads. While some audiobooks are very simple, with just a single voice actor reading the text of the book, others have higher production values, with different actors for

Many people enjoy multitasking by listening to podcasts or audiobooks while running errands, doing chores, or working on their laptops at the same time.

each character, background music, and even sound effects, which can make listening to an audiobook an entirely different experience from reading the same book in print.

The process of creating an audiobook is similar to that of recording an album. The engineer will work in a studio, recording, mixing, and mastering the audio. But not every audiobook is quite so straightforward.

One striking example of what is possible in the audiobook format is the seven-hour-long *Lincoln in the Bardo*, by George Saunders, (produced by Kelly Gildea), with its world record of 166 voice actors, including celebrities like Lena Dunham, Miranda July, Julianne Moore, and Susan Sarandon, whose voices were recorded in studios all over the country and then edited together over the course of three months. There aren't many mediums that allow you to be part of a project like that.

PREPARATION

It's hard to prepare for jobs that might not even exist yet, but it never hurts to keep your finger on the pulse. Try to keep up to date on new technology that is being developed and released by reading the news, blogs, and magazines and even by listening to podcasts. If you can become familiar with a new technology before it becomes widely known, you'll have a massive advantage in finding employment in that field.

In terms of video games, audiobooks, and podcasts, there are some universities that offer specialized courses in these areas (particularly in gaming), but the best way to gain experience is just to get involved yourself. Start your own podcast or produce one for your friends, record some audiobooks of books that are in the public domain, or offer to do the sound for a local developer's game. You'll learn a lot just by figuring it out as you go, and you'll be building your reel at the same time.

JOB OUTLOOK

It's impossible to know what the audio-engineering job market will look like in the future. New technologies are being developed every day, any one of which could drastically alter the audio industry. What we do know is that the number of jobs available in new audio fields is consistently increasing, so there are likely to be plenty of exciting opportunities in this changing industry in years to come.

Chapter six

SOUND IS EVERYWHERE, JOBS AREN'T

You've decided what sort of job you want, you've completed your education, and learned all the necessary skills, now all that's left is to start working at your dream job, right? Unfortunately, life isn't always that simple. Just because you're qualified

Most audio engineers start out as interns or assistants, which gives them the opportunity to learn from more experienced engineers.

for a job, doesn't mean you'll get it. The job you want might not even be available when you're ready for it. But there are a few things you can do to make the most of your job-hunting experience.

RÉSUMÉ AND REEL

While it is still important to have a traditional résumé, it often isn't enough to secure an audio-engineering job. Most employers are less interested in what you look like on paper and more concerned with what your audio sounds like. Because of this, it is important to have a reel of your work, as well as a list of your skills and accomplishments.

Your résumé should list all of your education, experience, and achievements related to audio. It should also go into detail about your specific skills and responsibilities. For instance, if you had a job at a movie theater and operated the speakers or archived the sound files, make sure you mention that. It also helps to outline your interests and say what sort of work you're looking for and what you hope to get out of a job, to give potential employers a better idea of who you are as a person. Many websites like LiveCareer, JobHero, and CVTips have advice and sample résumés.

Your reel, on the other hand, shouldn't include all the projects you've worked on. Instead it should showcase three or four of your very best pieces, considering the requirements of the position you're applying for. Although you're applying for a job in audio, it's often a good idea for your reel to

Make sure you get someone else to look over your résumé before you send it off. That person's feedback could be the difference between you getting a job or not.

include visuals as well. If you've engineered live performances for films or games, you can include the visuals that go along with your audio. Otherwise for the visual part, you can include the covers of albums you've worked on, as well as text identifying the name of the artist, when the audio was recorded, and the specific work you did on the project.

NETWORKING

As the old saying goes, it's not what you know, it's who you know. You could be the most qualified audio engineer to ever exist, but if no one knew who you were, you still wouldn't be able to secure a job. Working as an audio engineer means needing to have strong connections with artists, studio owners, record labels, and other engineers, as all of these people can help you book gigs.

For some people, the idea of networking can be very daunting, but it doesn't have to be as frightening as you imagine. Think of it this way: if you're part of the AV club at school, everyone else in the club is a contact and so is the teacher who supervises the club; when you're studying audio engineering at college, all of your classmates are contacts, as are your professors; any of your friends who are in bands or do anything creative involving audio are contacts; and anyone you've ever done a job with or for is another contact. If you add all those people up, you've probably already got a sizable network, so make sure to keep in touch with these people. They might be able to offer you a job one day.

If you're looking to expand your network even further, the next step is to put yourself into situations where you can meet people in the field. Join organizations like Sound Girls, the Audio Engineering Society, and the Game Audio Network Guild, and be an active member. Go to bars that have regular live music, and while you're there, talk to the sound person. Apply for internships, use them as opportunities to get to know the people already working in the industry, and ask as many questions as possible. Contact studios and ask if you can come in to visit and see how they do things. And remember, networking doesn't just lead to future jobs, it also provides opportunities for you to learn more about the industry and your craft.

GOING FREELANCE

If you've managed to build up a strong network of contacts in the industry but haven't been able to find a permanent position that fits your requirements, then you might want to consider working freelance. It can be tough to make a living as a freelance audio engineer unless you've already been in the industry for a while and have built up a significant client base, but securing a few contract jobs here and there can help you gain experience and potentially lead to more reliable work in the future.

The type of jobs you're able to pick up as a freelancer depends on the equipment you have available to you. If you don't have recording equipment, no band is going to hire you to record their album. They'll go to a studio and use the engineers there. So unless you have the large amount of capital necessary to set up your own studio, your freelance work will probably be limited to jobs where the equipment is provided, like engineering

(continued on the next page)

(continued from the previous page)

for touring bands or filling in at venues when the regular sound person isn't available.

Working freelance isn't right for everyone. Some people struggle with the lack of stability and operate better within the structure of a traditional job. But other people thrive in an environment in which they can be their own boss, choose what jobs they take on, and have flexible hours. You don't always know which type of person you are until you give freelancing a try.

Being able to work from the comfort of your own home is a big reason why many people choose to go freelance.

APPLYING FOR JOBS

When you're starting your career, it pays not to rule anything out. Consider every opportunity carefully. Even if what you really want to do is engineer heavy metal music, a job offer at a video-game studio may give you experience and contacts that will eventually help you reach your ultimate goal.

With that in mind, it is probably in your best interests to apply as widely as you can. Don't be too swayed by genre, pay, or location. Once you've built up some experience, you'll be able to find work that suits you better. But just because you're not being especially selective starting out, doesn't mean you shouldn't research the places you're applying to. In fact, you should find out as much as you can about the organizations you're applying to work for. Try to learn what they specialize in, what sort of equipment they use, and anything you can about the people who already work there. You can use this information to tailor your résumé, cover letter, and reel to this particular organization, giving you a much better chance at getting the job.

INTERVIEWING

Just as a traditional résumé often isn't enough to get you an audio-engineering job, the same is true of a traditional interview. While it's important to be able to sell yourself by speaking about your skills and previous experiences and how they have prepared you for this position, the employer may also want to see how you operate in the workplace and what your interactions with clients are like. In this case, the interview can become more of a tryout, in which you are required to enter the workplace and interact with the equipment. In these situations, it's important to stay calm, show them what you're comfortable doing, and ask questions about anything you're unsure of. The worst thing you can do is pretend you know what you're doing when you really have no idea. That will only make a bad impression and won't help you get the job.

Whatever the result, a job interview is always a helpful learning experience. The more interviews you have, the more practice you're getting. So even if you don't get the job, put it down as experience and keep trying!

Chapter seven

SURVIVING AS AN AUDIO ENGINEER

Getting a job isn't the end of the process; it's only the beginning. Now you've got a long career ahead of you, full of exciting projects, new challenges, and unexpected setbacks. Every career has its highs and lows, but if you know what's coming, the struggles might not hit you quite as hard.

DIFFERENT WORK ENVIRONMENTS

Not every audio engineer works in the same kind of environment. Some spend their days in recording studios, while others work out of news vans, and many work freelance, splitting their time between various different spaces like music venues, universities, hospitals, and anywhere else audio professionals are needed.

RECORDING STUDIO

This is where most people who dream of becoming audio engineers picture themselves working, behind

Even though you may be using the same skills, working as an in-house engineer at a theater is very different from working at a music festival.

the massive mixing desks, looking through the soundproof glass into the booth where a band is recording. It's easy to glorify this image, but working in a studio isn't always as amazing as you imagine it being. The job won't seem as glamorous when you're at work into the early hours of the morning because a band needs to get their album recorded by a deadline and they just can't seem to get this one track right.

Other things you need to consider when working in a studio include repetitive strain injuries (RSIs) and making sure you don't sit for too long, which can increase the risk of diabetes and heart attacks. Make sure you take regular breaks to stand up, stretch, and look after your body.

VENUES

The majority of venues have their own in-house audio engineers, who work with the various groups that use the venue to provide them with the sound they need. As well as music venues, sports arenas, colleges, libraries, and more employ their own audio engineers. This type of work requires strong social skills because as well as audio engineering, your role includes a significant amount of customer service. Not only do you have to make people sound good, you also have to leave them happy with their experience so that they'll return to use your venue again next time.

Recording audio out in nature comes with a lot more challenges than working in a controlled indoor environment.

ON THE ROAD

Some audio engineers don't have a single place of work because their work takes them to a new place every day. If you're engineering for a band on tour, you could be traveling all across the country or even the world. If you're the engineer for a news station, you might work out of a van, going from place to place with reporters.

WORKPLACE HARASSMENT AND ABUSE

It is a sad truth that not all workplaces are safe spaces for women. Kesha's lawsuit against her producer, Dr. Luke, for sexual assault (among other charges) received a huge amount of media attention, but gendered violence doesn't just affect artists. Producers and engineers are just as likely, if not more, to be on the receiving end. A 2016 study by the Equal Employment Opportunity Commission found that at least 25 percent of women report having experienced sexual harassment in the workplace and that it is more common in male-dominated industries.

You should never take a job in a workplace you don't feel comfortable in. Even if you don't experience obvious discrimination or harassment there, a feeling of unease will have a negative effect on your mental health. When possible, it is a good idea to find work at organizations that have a strong female presence, not only for your comfort, but also because women are more likely to understand and respond compassionately if you share your experiences with them.

In the end, the more women there are working in audio and in positions of power at studios and venues, the more of a positive working environment it will become for women.

This sort of work can be exhausting, as even when you're not actually engineering, you're still working. Packing and unpacking gear and traveling from place to place can take a toll on your body.

It's important to get rest when you can and to find regular time and space to get away from the work environment. Taking yourself to dinner and a movie can do wonders.

CONTINUED LEARNING

No matter how much you know about audio engineering and what sort of qualifications you have,

Attending conferences is a great way to stay in touch with the latest industry developments and build your list of audio engineering contacts.

you will learn a lot over the course of your career. This learning happens both on the technical side of engineering and the human side. Every job will teach you something about how to interact and work with other people. You will learn the quirks of the people you work with regularly and develop strategies for interacting with new clients, all of which will help you in your career.

You will also need to learn how to use new technology. The equipment used for audio engineering is constantly changing and developing. If you fall behind the curve, you'll begin losing out on jobs to people who are familiar with the latest technology. Because of this, many audio engineers take courses and attend conferences throughout their careers to make sure they remain at the cutting edge.

CREATING COMMUNITY

When working in a male-dominated industry like audio engineering, it's important to help and support other women who are in the same field. You will share many of the same struggles and be able to relate to each other's experiences. When you're first starting your career, reach out to other women who have been working in audio for longer than you. They will be able to teach you a lot, and finding good mentors can be a huge boost to your career. And once you've established yourself in the business, don't forget the help you received on your way. Pay it forward to

Being an audio engineer is a lot of hard work, but it can also be a lot of fun and lead to experiences you wouldn't have in any other field.

other young women who are entering the industry. By helping each other in this way, women can make the audio industry a more welcoming and inclusive space and find sustained success.

Glossary

AMPLIFIER An electronic device that increases the volume of audio.

AUDIOBOOK A recording of a book being read aloud.

AUDIO ENGINEER Someone who records, edits, mixes, or masters audio.

AUTOMATIC DIALOGUE REPLACEMENT The process of adding dialogue that wasn't recorded during filming to visuals.

AUTO-TUNE Technology that automatically corrects the pitch of audio.

BOOM A microphone attached to a pole, which allows it to be held as close to an actor as possible during filming without getting in the shot.

BROADCASTING Transmitting audio by either radio or television.

COMPRESSION An audio-editing technique that decreases the volume of loud sounds and increases the volume of quiet ones.

DIRECTIONAL MICROPHONE A microphone that records only sounds coming from a specific direction.

FOLEY The reproduction and recording of everyday human sounds, like footsteps, for inclusion in film and television. Named after the sound-effects artist Jack Foley.

LAVALIER A microphone that is attached to a speaker's clothing.

MASTERING The final step of processing recorded audio before distribution. It includes balancing the audio levels between different files and creating transitions between them.

MIXING The process of combining multiple audio tracks into a single file. It includes adjusting the volume of the tracks so that no one sound overpowers the others.

MONITORS Speakers that face musicians during a performance so that they know what they sound like.

MONO An audio recording where the same elements play out of all speakers.

PANNING A method of editing audio so that certain elements of a track come from certain speakers, rather than each speaker playing the exact same sound.

PODCAST An audio series that is automatically downloaded to your device whenever a new episode is published.

REEL A selection of audio you've worked on to show potential employers what you can do.

REVERB An echo effect that can be electronically applied to audio.

ROOM TONE The sound of the "silence" that is recorded at a particular location or space, when no dialogue is being spoken.

STEREO An audio recording in which different elements play out of left and right speakers.

SURROUND SOUND An audio recording in which different elements play out of a variety of speakers.

TAKES Attempts at recording a piece of audio. Sometimes it can take multiple takes to get the sound right.

TRACKING A method of sound recording that allows each sound to be recorded separately.

For More Information

Audio Engineering Society
551 Fifth Avenue, Suite 1225
New York, NY 10176
http://www.aes.org
Facebook: @AES.org
Instagram: @aes_org
Twitter: @AESorg
The Audio Engineering Society is the only professional society in the United States devoted exclusively to audio technology. It offers members a huge catalogue of resources.

Engineer Girl
National Academy of Engineering
500 Fifth Street NW, Room 1047
Washington, DC 20001
https://www.engineergirl.org
Twitter: @EngineerGirlNAE
This website is run by the National Academy of Engineering and designed to bring attention to engineering opportunities for girls and women.

Game Audio Network Guild
http://www.audiogang.org
Twitter: @audiogang
This organization provides networking and educational events to help audio professionals in the game industry to improve their craft.

The Noize Factory
151 Yonge Street, 11th Floor
Toronto, ON M5C 2W7
Canada
https://www.noizefaktory.com
This Canadian training and mentorship program is for people looking to pursue a career in audio. It offers one-on-one artist development.

Recording Arts Canada
390 Notre Dame West, Suite 320
Montréal, QC H2Y 1T9
Canada
https://recordingarts.com
Facebook: @Recording.Arts.Canada
Twitter: @Recording_Arts
Recording Arts Canada provides a world-class learning environment and aims to accelerate the careers of young people interested in audio.

Sound Girls
http://www.soundgirls.org
Facebook and Twitter: @SoundGirlsOrg
Instagram: @SoundGirls
Sound Girls is a network of women working in the audio industry whose mission is to inspire and empower the next generation of women in audio and build a supportive community for them.

Women's Audio Mission
542-544 Natoma Street, #C-1
San Francisco, CA 94103
https://www.womensaudiomission.org
Facebook: @womensaudiomission
Twitter: @womensaudio
This nonprofit organization is dedicated to the advancement of women and girls in the audio industry. It provides hands-on training, work experience, career counseling, and job training to more than 1,200 women and girls every year.

For Further Reading

Anniss, Matt. *Make a Podcast!* (Find Your Talent). Mankato, MN: Arcturus Publishing, 2013.

Cefrey, Holly. *Career Building Through Music, Video, and Software Mashups*. New York, NY: Rosen Publishing, 2008.

Cooper, Christopher. *The Basics of Sound* (Core Concepts). New York, NY: Rosen Publishing, 2015.

Culp, Jennifer. *Using Computer Science in Digital Music Careers* (Coding Your Passion). New York, NY: Rosen Publishing, 2018.

Fontichiaro, Kristin. *Speak Out! Creating Podcasts and Other Audio Recordings*. Ann Arbor, MI: Cherry Lake Publishing, 2013.

Furgang, Kathy, and Adam Furgang. *Internship & Volunteer Opportunities for People Who Love Music* (A Foot in the Door). New York, NY: Rosen Publishing, 2013.

Hasan, Heather. *How to Produce, Release, and Market Your Music* (Garage Bands). New York, NY: Rosen Publishing, 2012.

Hollar, Sherman. *Sound* (Introduction to Physics). Chicago, IL: Britannica, 2013.

Mooney, Carla. *Cool Careers Without College for People Who Love Music*. New York, NY: Rosen Publishing, 2014.

Rooney, Anne. *Audio Engineering and the Science of Soundwaves*. St. Catharines, Ontario: Crabtree Publishing Company, 2013.

Bibliography

Bartlett, Bruce. "The Beginners Guide to Taking Charge of the Sound Check." ProSoundWeb, April 2015. https://www.prosoundweb.com/channels/church/the_beginners_guide_to_taking_charge_of_the_soundcheck.

Bent, Louise. "Becoming a Recording Engineer." CareersInMusic. Retrieved November 29, 2017. https://www.careersinmusic.com/recording-engineer.

Bureau of Labor Statistics. "Broadcast and Sound Engineering Technicians." October 2017. https://www.bls.gov/ooh/media-and-communication/broadcast-and-sound-engineering-technicians.htm.

Bureau of Labor Statistics. "Occupational Employment and Wages, Sound Engineering Technicians." March 31, 2017. https://www.bls.gov/oes/current/oes274014.htm.

Ciccarelli, Stephanie. "History of Podcasting." Voices. Retrieved December 1, 2017. https://www.voices.com/resources/articles/podcasting/history-of-podcasting.

Edison Research. "The Podcast Consumer." Retrieved December 1, 2017. http://www.edisonresearch.com/wp-content/uploads/2017/04/Podcast-Consumer-2017.pdf.

Estrada, Louie. "As a Female Broadcast Engineer, Pioneer Rose Above the Prejudice." *Washington Post*, March 28, 2004. https://www.washingtonpost.com/archive/local/2004/03/28

/as-a-female-broadcast-engineer-pioneer-rose-above-the-prejudice/383f6c1c-b5b8-4fee-a0ec-a12eef5d2936/?utm_term=.1fefdc8c97f9.

Feldblum, Chai R., and Victoria A. Lipnic. "Select Taskforce on the Study of Harassment in the Workplace." Equal Employment Opportunity Commission, June 2016. https://www.eeoc.gov/eeoc/task_force/harassment/upload/report.pdf.

Lanzendorfer, Joy. "Why Aren't There More Women Working in Audio?" *The Atlantic,* August 30, 2017. https://www.theatlantic.com/entertainment/archive/2017/08/why-arent-there-more-women-working-in-audio/537663.

Locke, Charley. "The 7-Hour, 166-Person Audiobook That Feels Like a Movie." *Wired*, February 14, 2017. https://www.wired.com/2017/02/george-saunders-bardo-white-house-audiobook.

Loh, Genevieve Sarah. "Singaporean Ai-Ling Lee Still a Winner Despite Losing the Oscar." Channel NewsAsia, February 27, 2017. http://www.channelnewsasia.com/news/lifestyle/singaporean-ai-ling-lee-still-a-winner-despite-losing-the-oscar-7601460.

Mayzes, Rob. "Order of Operations: The Phases of Audio Post-Production for Video Projects." Envato Tuts+, July 6, 2016. https://photography.tutsplus.com/tutorials/understanding-the-phases-of-audio-post-production-for-video--cms-26688.

Milliot, Jim. "Audiobook Sales Up Again in 2016, Posting Double-Digit Gains." *Publishers Weekly*, June 7, 2017. https://www.publishersweekly.com/pw/by-topic/industry-news/audio-books/article/73917-audiobooks-posted-double-digit-gains-in-sales-output.html.

Schmidt, Brian. "Analysis: The Game Audio Gender Gap." Game Sound Con, August 2016. https://www.gamesoundcon.com/single-post/2016/08/28/Analysis-The-Game-Audio-Gender-Gap.

Smith, John. "Interview with Emily Ridgway." GANG, April 2011. http://www.audiogang.org/interview-with-emily-ridgway.

Society of Broadcast Engineers, The. "Why Be Certified?" Retrieved December 2, 2017. http://www.sbe.org/sections/cert_index.php.

Studio Pros. "Music Mixing: What It Is, and Why It's Important." July 29, 2010. https://studiopros.com/music-mixing.

Thanki, Juli. "Shani Gandhi Soars Behind the Soundboard." *Tennessean*, February 11, 2017. http://www.tennessean.com/story/entertainment/music/2017/02/11/shani-gandhi-soars-behind-soundboard/97246692.

Tucker, April. "From 'Girl Engineer' to Re-Recording Mixer—Sherry Klein." SoundGirls. Retrieved November 29, 2017. http://www.soundgirls.org/from-girl-engineer-to-re-recording-mixer-sherry-klein.

Index

ABOUT THE AUTHOR

Jackson Nieuwland is a writer, editor, and librarian from New Zealand. They have an MA in creative writing from the International Institute of Modern Letters. When they were a teenager they wanted to be a rapper, so they bought a microphone and a secondhand mixer to hook up to their computer so they could record their songs in their own home. They haven't done much recording since then, but they often think about starting their own podcast or YouTube channel.

PHOTO CREDITS

Cover wavebreakmedia/Shutterstock.com; cover, interior pages (circuit board illustration) © iStockphoto.com/Vladgrin; pp. 4–5 Peter Muller/Cultura/Getty Images; p. 9 Peathegee /Blend Images/Getty Images; p. 12 Jacomo/Shutterstock.com; p. 14 Janelle Lugge/Shutterstock.com; p. 17 Nejron Photo /Shutterstock.com; p. 20 Alberto E. Rodriguez/WireImage /Getty Images; p. 24 Jesse Grant/Getty Images; p. 27 bjones27 /E+/Getty Images; p. 29 Future Music Magazine/Future /Getty Images; p. 32 Hill Street Studios/Blend Images /Getty Images; p. 35 gnepphoto/Shutterstock.com; p. 36 Stephen Dunn/Getty Images; p. 39 Tyler Olson/Shutterstock.com; p. 43 Chesnot/Getty Images; p. 45 JHPhoto/Alamy Stock Photo; p. 46 Arcady/Shutterstock.com; p. 48 Bloom Productions /Taxi/Getty Images; pp. 51, 53 Hero Images/Getty Images; p. 56 AleksandarGeorgiev/E+/Getty Images; p. 60 Arctic-Images/ Corbis Documentary/Getty Images; p. 62 Charlie Sperring/ Shutterstock.com; p. 64 Klaus Vedfelt/Taxi/Getty Images; p. 66 Mondadori Portfolio/Getty Images.

Design and Layout: Nicole Russo-Duca; Editor: Rachel Aimee; Photo Researcher: Karen Huang